Daniel Plays Ball

adapted by Maggie Testa

based on the screenplay "Daniel Plays Ball" written by

Eva Steele-Saccio

poses and layouts by Jason Fruchter

Ready-to-Read

Simon Spotlight

New York   London   Toronto   Sydney   New Delhi

Hi, neighbor!
We are playing
animal ball.

Whoever throws the ball, picks an animal.

Then we all make its sound.

Miss Elaina picks a dog.

We all say . . .

Miss Elaina throws the ball to Prince Wednesday.

Grr. I missed the ball.

"Keep trying. You will get better," says Prince Tuesday.

"Quack, quack, quack!"

Prince Tuesday throws
the ball to Miss Elaina.

She catches the ball.

Miss Elaina throws
the ball to me.

Grr. I miss it again!

"Keep trying. You will get better," says Prince Tuesday.

Miss Elaina throws
the ball to me again.

I watch the ball.

Then I hug the ball.

"Nice catch,"

says Prince Tuesday.

Daniel Gets Scared

adapted by Maggie Testa
based on the screenplay "A Stormy Day"
written by Wendy Harris
poses and layouts by Jason Fruchter

Ready-to-Read

Simon Spotlight
New York   London   Toronto   Sydney   New Delhi

We like to jump
in puddles together.

"Time to go inside," calls Mom.

"There is something I do when I am scared," says Mom.

Books make him happy.
He feels a little
less scared now.

Boom!

We hear more thunder.

It scares us again.

"When you are scared, close your eyes and think of something happy," I said.

We feel less scared now.

Daniel Feels Left Out

adapted by Maggie Testa

based on the screenplay written by Becky Friedman
and Angela C. Santomero

poses and layouts by Jason Fruchter

Ready-to-Read

Simon Spotlight

New York London Toronto Sydney New Delhi

My dad and I are on our way home for dinner.

Katerina and O
are playing outside.

I say hi.

I want to play too.

He tells me that it is okay to feel sad.

It helps to talk about your feelings!

It is okay to feel sad sometimes.

Friends Help Each Other

adapted by Farrah McDoogle

based on the screenplay "Friends Help Each Other" written by Wendy Harris

poses and layouts by Jason Fruchter

Ready-to-Read

Simon Spotlight

New York   London   Toronto   Sydney   New Delhi

Hi, neighbor!

Today I am playing

with Katerina Kittycat.

"Meow, Meow!
Do you want to have a
tea party?"
asks Katerina.

"Let me get a chair for you!" says Katerina.

Everything falls on the floor!

"Maybe Daniel can help!" says Henrietta.

"Teatime!"
says Katerina.

Oh no!

Katerina spills the tea.

I can help clean up
the tea!

Friends help each other, yes they do!

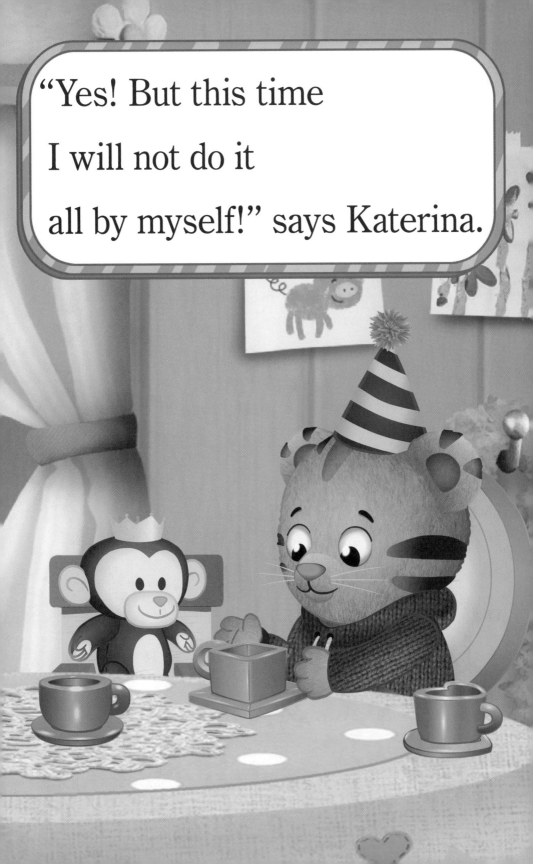

"Will you help me pour?" asks Katerina.

I am happy I helped
my friend today!
Ugga Mugga!

Daniel Visits the Library

adapted by Maggie Testa

based on the screenplay "Calm for Storytime"

written by Wendy Harris

poses and layouts by Jason Fruchter

Ready-to-Read

Simon Spotlight

New York   London   Toronto   Sydney   New Delhi

Hi, neighbor!
We are going to the
library for storytime.

At last it is storytime!

Prince Wednesday hops like a frog.

We listen to the story.

X the Owl finishes
the story.

"The end," he says.

Storytime is over. Now we can go outside and play.

Daniel Plays at School

adapted by Daphne Pendergrass

based on the screenplay "Problem Solver Daniel"

written by Becky Friedman

poses and layouts by Jason Fruchter

Ready-to-Read

Simon Spotlight

New York   London   Toronto   Sydney   New Delhi

"What should we do?"
We ask Teacher Harriet.

She says, "Try to solve the problem yourself. You will feel proud."